JE

# The Boy Who Cried Wolf

Retold by BLAKE HOENA
Illustrations by FLAVIA SORRENTINO
Music by MARK OBLINGER

CANTATA
LEARNING

# CANTATA LEARNING

Published by Cantata Learning
1710 Roe Crest Drive
North Mankato, MN 56003
www.cantatalearning.com

**Library of Congress Cataloging-in-Publication Data**
Names: Hoena, B. A., author. | Sorrentino, Flavia, illustrator. | Oblinger,
    Mark, composer. | Aesop.
Title: The boy who cried wolf / retold by Blake Hoena ; illustrated by Flavia
    Sorrentino ; music by Mark Oblinger.
Description: North Mankato, MN : Cantata Learning, [2018] | Series: Classic
    fables in rhythm and rhyme | Summary: A modern song retells the fable of
    the boy tending sheep who thinks it a fine joke to cry "wolf" and watch
    the people come running, until the day a wolf is really there and no one
    answers his call. Includes a brief introduction to Aesop, sheet music,
    glossary, discussion questions, and further reading.
Identifiers: LCCN 2017017522 (print) | LCCN 2017035541 (ebook) | ISBN
    9781684101498 (ebook) | ISBN 9781684101221 (hardcover : alk. paper) | ISBN
    9781684101856 (paperback : alk. paper)
Subjects: | CYAC: Behavior--Songs and music. | Fables. | Folklore. | Songs.
Classification: LCC PZ8.3.H667 (ebook) | LCC PZ8.3.H667 Boy 2018 (print) |
    DDC 398.2 [E] --dc23
LC record available at https://lccn.loc.gov/2017017522

Book design and art direction, Tim Palin Creative
Editorial direction, Kellie M. Hultgren
Music direction, Elizabeth Draper
Music arranged and produced by Mark Oblinger

Printed in the United States of America in North Mankato, Minnesota.
122017            0378CGS18

ACCESS THE MUSIC!

SCAN CODE WITH MOBILE APP

CANTATALEARNING.COM

# TIPS TO SUPPORT LITERACY AT HOME

## WHY READING AND SINGING WITH YOUR CHILD IS SO IMPORTANT

Daily reading with your child leads to increased academic achievement. Music and songs, specifically rhyming songs, are a fun and easy way to build early literacy and language development. Music skills correlate significantly with both phonological awareness and reading development. Singing helps build vocabulary and speech development. And reading and appreciating music together is a wonderful way to strengthen your relationship.

### READ AND SING EVERY DAY!

## TIPS FOR USING CANTATA LEARNING BOOKS AND SONGS DURING YOUR DAILY STORY TIME

1.  As you sing and read, point out the different words on the page that rhyme. Suggest other words that rhyme.

2.  Memorize simple rhymes such as Itsy Bitsy Spider and sing them together. This encourages comprehension skills and early literacy skills.

3.  Use the questions in the back of each book to guide your singing and storytelling.

4.  Read the included sheet music with your child while you listen to the song. How do the music notes correlate to the words of the song?

5.  Sing along on the go and at home. Access music by scanning the QR code on each Cantata book, or by using the included CD. You can also stream or download the music for free to your computer, smartphone, or mobile device.

Devoting time to daily reading shows that you are available for your child. Together, you are building language, literacy, and listening skills.

Have fun reading and singing!

**Aesop** was a storyteller who wrote hundreds of stories called **fables**. Each of these short tales taught a **moral**, or lesson.

In this fable, a bored shepherd boy yells, "Wolf!" just to get the attention of the **villagers**. When they find out that there is not any danger, the villagers get upset. What lesson can be learned from the boy who cried wolf?

Turn the page to find out. Remember to sing along!

There once was a shepherd boy, shepherd boy, shepherd boy.

There once was a shepherd boy who got tired watching sheep.

Oh, the boy was bored so he played a joke, played a joke.

He jumped up and cried, "Help me! A wolf is chasing the sheep!"

The villagers ran up and shrieked, "Where's the wolf? Where's the wolf?"

When they learned the truth they screeched, "Don't cry 'wolf' when there's none."

The boy just laughed, "Ho, ho, ho!
Ha, ha, ha! Ho, ho, ho!"

The villagers all stomped off home.
But that shepherd was not done.

The boy got bored again, so he played a joke, another joke.

He cried out again, "Help me! A wolf is eating the sheep!"

The villagers ran up and shrieked,
"Where's the wolf? Where's the wolf?"

When they learned the truth they screeched,
"No wolves are getting the sheep!"

But then one day, the shepherd boy really saw a wolf, and what do you think happened?

The shepherd boy leaped up and yelped,
"There's a wolf, a big bad wolf!"

But no one came out to help.

So the wolf got away with the sheep!

So the moral of our story goes:
If you tell lies, lots of lies,
then no one will ever know
if you can be believed.

Oh, by telling lies, lots of lies, then no one will ever know if you can be believed.

# SONG LYRICS
## The Boy Who Cried Wolf

There once was a shepherd boy,
shepherd boy, shepherd boy.
There once was a shepherd boy
who got tired watching sheep.

Oh, the boy was bored so he
played a joke, played a joke.
He jumped up and cried, "Help me!
A wolf is chasing the sheep!"

The villagers ran up and shrieked,
"Where's the wolf? Where's the wolf?"
When they learned the truth they screeched,
"Don't cry 'wolf' when there's none."

The boy just laughed, "Ho, ho, ho!
Ha, ha, ha! Ho, ho, ho!"
The villagers all stomped off home.
But that shepherd was not done.

The boy got bored again, so he
played a joke, another joke.
He cried out again, "Help me!
A wolf is eating the sheep!"

The villagers ran up and shrieked,
"Where's the wolf? Where's the wolf?"
When they learned the truth they screeched,
"No wolves are getting the sheep!"

But then one day, the shepherd boy really saw a
    wolf, and what do you think happened?

The shepherd boy leaped up and yelped,
"There's a wolf, a big bad wolf!"
But no one came out to help.
So the wolf got away with the sheep!

So the moral of our story goes:
If you tell lies, lots of lies,
then no one will ever know
if you can be believed.

Oh, by telling lies, lots of lies,
then no one will ever know
if you can be believed.

# The Boy Who Cried Wolf

**Rock and Roll/Zydeco Roots**
Mark Oblinger

**Chorus 1-2**

There once was a shep-herd boy, shep-herd boy, shep-herd boy. There once was a shep-herd boy who got tired watch-ing sheep.

**Verse**

1. Oh, the boy was bored so he played a joke, played a joke. He jumped up and cried, "Help me! A wolf is chasing the sheep!"

**Verse 2**
The villagers ran up and shrieked,
"Where's the wolf? Where's the wolf?"
When they learned the truth they screeched,
"Don't cry 'wolf' when there's none."

**Chorus**
The boy just laughed, "Ho, ho, ho!
Ha, ha, ha! Ho, ho, ho!"
The villagers all stomped off home.
But that shepherd was not done.

**Verse 3**
The boy got bored again, so he
played a joke, another joke.
He cried out again, "Help me!
A wolf is eating the sheep!"

**Verse 4**
The villagers ran up and shrieked,
"Where's the wolf? Where's the wolf?"
When they learned the truth they screeched,
"No wolves are getting the sheep!"

**Interlude**

"But then one day, the shepherd boy really saw a wolf, and what do you think happened?"

**Chorus 3**

The shep-herd boy leaped up and yelped, "There's a wolf, a big bad wolf!" But no one came out to help. So the wolf got a-way with the sheep!

**Outro**

So the mor-al of our sto-ry goes: If you tell lies, lots of lies, then no one will ev-er know if you can be be-lieved. Oh, by tell-ing lies, lots of lies,

then no one will ev-er know if you can be be-lieved.

# GLOSSARY

**Aesop**—a legendary storyteller who is said to have lived in ancient Greece around 600 BCE

**fables**—short stories that often have animal characters and teach a lesson

**moral**—a lesson, often found in a fable or story

**villagers**—someone who lives in a very small town

# GUIDED READING ACTIVITIES

1. After reading this story, what does the saying "Don't cry wolf" mean to you?

2. The boy got bored while watching the sheep. Is there something else he could have done to keep from being bored? What do you do when you are bored?

3. Sheep are one of many kinds of animals that farmers raise. What are some other animals you might see on a farm? Draw a picture of a farm with all of the different animals that you listed.

## TO LEARN MORE

Adams, Elizabeth, and Daniel Howarth. *The Boy Who Cried Wolf*. New York: Crabtree, 2012.

Borgert–Spaniol, Megan. *Mary Had a Little Lamb*. North Mankato, MN: Cantata Learning, 2015.

Hoena, Blake. *The Tortoise and the Hare*. North Mankato, MN: Cantata Learning, 2018.

Strauss, Holden. *Wolves*. New York: PowerKids, 2017.